Text copyright © 1998 by Sheridan Cain
Illustrations copyright © 1998 by Tanya Linch

This 2004 edition published by Backpack Books,
by arrangement with Magi Publications, London.

Backpack Books
122 Fifth Avenue, New York, NY 10011

ISBN 0-7607-5979-0

Printed and bound in Singapore

04 05 06 07 08 [Imago] 10 9 8 7 6 5 4 3 2 1

First published in Great Britain 1998 by
Little Tiger Press, an imprint of Magi Publications, London

Sheridan Cain and Tanya Linch have asserted their rights
to be identified as the author and illustrator of this work
under the Copyright, Designs and Patents Act, 1988.

For my good friends,
Sue, Liz, and Irene
~ S. C.

For Aaron
~ T. L.

Look Out
for the
Big Bad Fish!

by **Sheridan Cain**

Pictures by **Tanya Linch**

BACKPACKBOOKS

·

NEW YORK

Tadpole swam in and out of the lily pads. It was warm, and he was having a wonderful time splishing and splashing.

"Hello, Tadpole," said Mother Frog
as she flopped onto a nearby lily pad.
"What a beautiful summer day!"

"What's summer, Mom?" asked
Tadpole.

"Summer is when it's warm,"
she said. "It's the best time for
frogs to leap and jump."

Boing

jumped Mother
Frog. She hopped
high into the air,
somersaulted,
and landed
with a PLOP!

"I bet *I* can do that," said Tadpole, and he tried to leap onto the lily pad where his mother sat. But all he could do was splish and splash.

"Mom, why can't I jump like you?" asked
Tadpole.

"Oh, you will, Tadpole," said Mother Frog.

"But I want to jump *now*," said Tadpole.

"When you are a little older, you will," said
his mother.

Disappointed, Tadpole swam off downstream.

"Come back soon, Tadpole!" called Mother Frog. "And look out for the Big Bad Fish!"

Tadpole wriggled his way to the edge of the
stream. Here among the buttercups it was safe.
"Hello," said a voice nearby. Tadpole looked
up and saw a woolly face with a smudgy nose.

"Hello," said Tadpole.

"Who are you?"

"I'm Lamb," said the woolly face.

"Can you jump?" asked Tadpole.

"You bet I can!" said Lamb. "Watch this!"

Boing

jumped Lamb.

"Phew!" said
Tadpole. "I wish
I could jump like that."

"Oh, you will, Tadpole,"
said Lamb. "When you are
a little older, you will."

"But I want to
jump *now*," cried
Tadpole, and he swam
sadly home.

A few days later, Tadpole went
downstream again. He stopped to rest
where the water violets tickled his belly.
    "Hello," said a voice above him. Tadpole
looked up and saw a twitchy nose and the
largest pair of ears he'd ever seen.
    "Hello," said Tadpole. "Who are you?"
    "I'm Rabbit," said the animal with the
twitchy nose.

                    "Can you jump?" asked Tadpole.
                    "Can I jump?" said Rabbit.
                            "Watch this!"

Boing

jumped Rabbit.

"Oh my," said Tadpole. "I wish I could jump like that."

"Oh, you will, Tadpole," said Rabbit. "When you are a little older, you will."

"But I want to jump *now*," wailed Tadpole, and he swam home.

Several days later, Tadpole went exploring again. This time he stopped where the giant cattails wobbled in the wind.

"Hello," said a voice in his ear. Tadpole looked around. He saw a pair of bug eyes and two springy legs.

"Hello," said Tadpole. "Who are you?"

"I'm Grasshopper," said the bug-eyed creature.

"Can you jump?" asked Tadpole.

"Of course," said Grasshopper. "Watch this!"

Boing

jumped
Grasshopper.

"Wow!" said Tadpole. "I wish I could jump like that."

"Oh, you will, Tadpole," said Grasshopper. "When you are a little older, you will."

"But I want to jump *now*," wept Tadpole, and he swam home.

The next time Tadpole went out,
he swam farther than he ever had before.
The stream widened, and the water became deep.

"Hello," said a low voice beneath him. Tadpole
looked down and saw a pair of huge, rubbery lips.

"Hello," said Tadpole. "Who are you?"

"I'm the Big Bad Fish!" boomed the rubbery-
lipped creature.

"C-Can you j-jump?" stuttered Tadpole.

"No, BUT I *DO* EAT TADPOLES!"
said the Big Bad Fish.

Boing

jumped Tadpole.

Tadpole leapt higher than Lamb.
He leapt higher than Rabbit. He even
leapt higher than Grasshopper.
He leapt all the way back home
to the lily pads.

"Look, Mom," said Tadpole,
"I *can* jump!"
Tadpole's mother smiled and
said, "What did I tell you,
Little Frog?"